DORLING KINDERSLEY *CLASSICS*

A CHRISTMAS CAROL

Dorling Kindersley

LONDON, NEW YORK, SYDNEY, DELHI,
PARIS, MUNICH and JOHANNESBURG

A NEW ABRIDGMENT FOR YOUNG READERS, BASED ON DICKENS' OWN ABRIDGMENT

Art Editor Lisa Lanzarini
Project Editor David Pickering
Senior Editor Marie Greenwood
US Editor Kristin Ward
Senior Designer Jane Thomas
Research Fergus Day
Production Katy Holmes
Managing Art Editor Chris Fraser
Picture Research Louise Thomas
DTP Designer Kim Browne
Consultant Shona McKellar

First American Edition, 1997
Paperback edition published 2000
4 6 8 10 9 7 5 3
Published in the United States by DK Publishing, Inc.
375 Hudson Street, New York, New York 10014
Copyright © 1997 Dorling Kindersley Limited

Library of Congress Cataloging-in-Publication Data
Dickens, Charles, 1812-1870.
  A Christmas carol/by Charles Dickens; illustrated by Andrew Wheatcroft.--1st
American ed.
    p. cm. -- (Dorling Kindersley read and listen)
Includes an audio tape featuring a reading of the text with special effects and music.
Summary: a miser learns the true meaning of Christmas when three ghostly visitors
review his past and foretell his future. Illustrated notes throughout the text explain the
historical background of the story.
  ISBN 0-7894-6246-X (pbk./audio tape) -- ISBN 0-7894 6363-6 (pbk./CD)
  [1. Christmas--Fiction. 2. Ghosts--Fiction. 3. England--Fiction.] I. Wheatcroft,
Andrew, ill. II. Title. III. Series.
PZ7.D55 Cew 2000
[Fic]--dc21
                                    99-086030
Color reproduction by Mullis Morgan
Printed and bound in China by L.Rex Printing Co., Ltd.

For our complete
catalog visit
www.dk.com

DORLING KINDERSLEY CLASSICS

A CHRISTMAS CAROL

CHARLES
DICKENS

Abridged by
SHONA MCKELLAR

A Dorling Kindersley Book

Illustrated by
ANDREW
WHEATCROFT

CONTENTS

Ebenezer
Scrooge

Jacob
Marley

The
Ghost of
Christmas
Past

The
Ghost of
Christmas
Present

The Ghost of
Christmas Yet
To Come

INTRODUCTION 5

DICKENS' LONDON 6

RICH AND POOR 8

One
MARLEY'S GHOST 10

Two
THE FIRST OF THE THREE SPIRITS 22

CHRISTMAS IN SCROOGE'S DAY 30

Three
THE SECOND OF THE THREE SPIRITS 32

Four
THE LAST OF THE SPIRITS 48

Five
THE END OF IT 56

CHARLES DICKENS 60

A CHRISTMAS CAROL 62

INTRODUCTION

WHEN DICKENS WROTE *A Christmas Carol* in 1843, he was burning to strike a "sledgehammer" blow for the poor. Britain then was a much harsher, crueller place than it is today. Extreme poverty was widespread. In London, there were terrible slums; for the poorer classes, the average age of death was 22. Dickens originally set out to write "An appeal to the People of England, on behalf of the Poor Man's Child", then thought of a story that would have a greater impact.

This Eyewitness Classic edition recreates the context of *A Christmas Carol*; the harsher, darker London about which Dickens wrote. It shows how the story of Scrooge reflected its author's views of his country's needs.

Scrooge, who values only money and has no love for anyone, embodies what Dickens most hated in the spirit of his age. The Ghosts' antidote to Scrooge's selfishness – the "spirit of Christmas", of love, joy, and care for others – is also Dickens' medicine for his country's divisions and injustice. As the Ghosts try to convert Scrooge to kindness, Dickens tried to convert his readers, to persuade them to practise the spirit of Christmas, not just at Christmas but all the year round.

The idyllic Christmas scenes that Dickens painted – very different from the reality most people experienced – were so enchanting that they became a universal picture of Christmas as it should be. Dickens set out to help the poor, and created a story so powerful that it defined the modern idea of Christmas.

Bob Cratchit

Mrs Cratchit

Tiny Tim

Scrooge's nephew

Scrooge's niece, by marriage

The Scrooges of London had everything their own way. They could pay their workers what they liked and fire them when they liked. Even so, any sort of job was better than none. There was no government help for the unemployed. Those who lost their work might even starve.

Ebenezer Scrooge

The Royal Exchange, a place for businessmen to meet and trade

Jobs in London

Many rich businessmen such as Scrooge made their money at the Royal Exchange (above). Their businesses were supported by ever-growing armies of poorly-paid clerical workers (below). A typical clerical worker received about £80 a year, just enough to support a family and rent a house. Scrooge pays his clerk Bob Cratchit half as much.

Clerks working at the Bank of England.

Ceaseless work

Many people worked twelve hours a day, six days a week. The only days off were Sundays, May Day, and Christmas Day. Employers did not have to let their employees off even for these. Many poor workers – domestic servants and factory workers, for example – had to work on Christmas Day. Scrooge resents giving Bob Cratchit even Christmas Day off.

In the painting *Work* (above), by Ford Madox Brown, different figures represent different forms of work and idleness. Dickens knew that England's wealth was created by the work of poor men and women such as those in this picture.

F ew people knew London as well as Dickens. He saw the great wealth that businessmen such as Scrooge were amassing, and he saw the overcrowding, the dirt, the unrelenting toil, and the disease that were the lot of most Londoners. Unfortunately, few other well-off people shared Dickens' concern. In *A Christmas Carol*, and his other books, he tried to make his readers understand how hard life was for the working poor, and how horrible it was for London's vast underclass of jobless, often homeless people.

Much of today's London was built in the 19th century

London was full of dark alleys and lanes

Coffee stall

Street conjurer performing

There were thousands of cab drivers

Many street-sellers were children

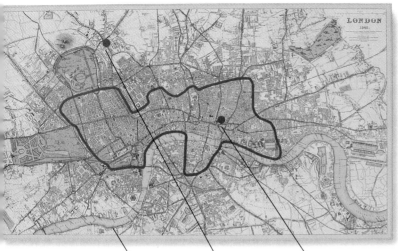

Dickens' city

Dickens is forever linked with London. All his life he loved to explore the city. By the time he was 15 years old he knew it well, both rich areas and poor. He continued to wander through it, by day and night, until the end of his life. London was his inspiration, his stories are full of its restless energy, and he made his city live in words as no one else has done.

London's Fleet Street in 1848

Exploding city

Throughout the 1800s London grew very rapidly. The map shows London in 1843; the red line shows the edge of the city in 1812, the year of Dickens' birth.

The Thames

Camden, where the Cratchits live, a poor but respectable district

This is the business district, called the City, where Scrooge lives and works

The worst slums were in the centre of London.

Working children

The streets were so filthy that people paid crossing-sweepers to sweep ahead of them as they crossed the street. Many children worked in such harsh jobs. Some children started work when they were as young as five.

A child crossing-sweeper

The smells of the city

Many foreign visitors to London commented that the overpowering smell was the smell of horse dung. There were thousands of horse-drawn omnibuses, cabs, carriages, and carts, but poor folk like Bob Cratchit and the young Dickens had to walk to work.

An 1847 horse-drawn omnibus

A blind boot-lace seller

A flower-seller

Costermongers sold fish, fruit, and vegetables

The London streets

London's streets were crowded, noisy, and very dirty. Almost anything was bought and sold, from pies and coffee to birds' nests and used clothing. There were street musicians, artists, conjurers, actors, and trained animals. The atmosphere of the streets, with buyers and sellers and entertainers and rich and poor all jumbled together, was perhaps more like some modern third-world cities than modern London.

A crippled bird-seller

INDUSTRIAL CITY

London was known as "the Fever Patch". It was the first big industrial city in the world, and it was extremely polluted and unhealthy. Diseases spread very quickly. There were four cholera epidemics in Dickens' lifetime, and regular outbreaks of typhoid, scarlet fever, and other illnesses. The River Thames was very busy and very polluted, and it smelt terrible. Two hundred open sewers ran into it, and half the population of London took their water straight out of it, for cooking, washing, and drinking.

RICH AND POOR

Poor children

In *A Christmas Carol*, Dickens shows us a cross-section of London society, from the very rich to the very poor, at the time of year when the gulf between rich and poor was most visible and felt most deeply. In the story, Christmas is described as the "time, of all others, when Want is keenly felt, and Abundance rejoices". The rich could look forward to resting, feasting, and receiving presents. The working poor would have Christmas Day off, if they were lucky, and might scrape together some sort of special meal. For the very poor, Christmas was just another day.

Wealthy people changed into evening dress for dinner

The fortunate few

Well-off people such as Scrooge's nephew and niece had servants to cook and clean for them, and do their dirty and rough work. They did not have to worry about money.

The working poor

The Cratchits represent an ever-growing class of struggling, poor working people. London's population more than doubled between 1800 and 1843, so there were more and more of them. As well as poverty, ill-health was a great worry for them, especially their children's ill-health: in 1839, almost half the funerals in London were for children under the age of 10.

An overcrowded street in Covent Garden, central London

HOUSING

In the poorest areas, some of which were right in the centre of London, families of up to eight people lived in a single room. Others, including many children, lived and died in the streets.

Dickens showed his concern for the poor in many books; these poor characters come from Oliver Twist.

A wealthy businessman

Grand houses

Rich people usually lived in large town houses (below), with small armies of servants to look after them. Scrooge preferred to live alone in the City, the business district, near his work and his money.

Poor family, 1840s

Looking respectable was very important to many Victorian people and a hat or bonnet was seen as essential

Clothes were mended and re-used many times

Clothes for children could be made from old, worn out adults' clothes

Rich family, 1840s

Waistcoats and cravats were made of silk or satin, imported from China; they were a colourful addition to a gentleman's outfit

Household servants had to be smartly dressed in practical uniforms

FOOD

For well-off families, regular and lavish meals were a sign of prosperity. At the other end of the social scale, many very poor people had to live on scraps of food or handouts from others.

A prosperous family's Christmas meal, c.1840

Children waiting for scraps of fish at a street market

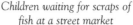

A boring diet

For many poorer people, Christmas was the one time in the year when they might eat special food. For the rest of the year, bread and potatoes were the main foods.

No rest for servants

Servants worked long hours and would often not even get Christmas Day off work. Other poor workers, such as Martha Cratchit, a milliner (hat maker), had to work on the morning of Christmas Day.

A maid would wash and press her mistress' clothes, sometimes even helping her to dress

Businessman, 1840s

Poor children

There were thousands of children like the Cratchits' poor, frail Tiny Tim. In unhealthy London, very many children were sickly or even died young. Few poor children had the chance of an education. Dickens campaigned on behalf of the "ragged schools", which tried to help the poorest of the poor.

Men's clothes were quite sombre in Scrooge's day

A top hat was always worn in the city

Women wore tight-fitting dresses with wide, bell-shaped skirts

Businessmen

A Christmas Carol is set in the early part of what is called "the Victorian era" of English history, named after Queen Victoria, who reigned 1837–1901. It was a time when businessmen such as Scrooge could make spectacular fortunes very quickly. Dickens fought to make them share their wealth.

A painting of 1849 showing poor people queuing outside a workhouse

Workhouses

Poor people who had no other means of support had to go to a workhouse. Here, people worked hard for basic food and shelter. A few years before *A Christmas Carol* was written, Dickens had fiercely attacked workhouses in his novel *Oliver Twist*.

Coats were tight fitting, as were trousers

Nobody ever stopped him
in the street to say,
with gladsome
looks, "My dear
Scrooge, how
are you?"

One

MARLEY'S GHOST

MARLEY WAS DEAD. There is no doubt whatever about that. The register of his burial was signed by the clergyman, the clerk, and the undertaker. Scrooge signed it. Old Marley was as dead as a doornail.

Scrooge knew he was dead? Of course he did. Scrooge and he were partners for I don't know how many years. Scrooge was his sole executor, his sole administrator, his sole friend, his sole mourner. There is no doubt that Marley was dead.

Scrooge never painted out Old Marley's name, however. There it stood, years afterwards, above the warehouse door: Scrooge and Marley. The firm was known as Scrooge and Marley. Sometimes people new to the business called Scrooge Scrooge, and sometimes Marley. He answered to both names. It was all the same to him.

Oh! But he was a tight-fisted hand at the grindstone, was Scrooge! A squeezing, wrenching, grasping, scraping, clutching, covetous old sinner! The cold within him froze his old features, nipped his pointed nose, shrivelled his cheek, stiffened his gait; made his eyes red, his thin lips blue.

Nobody ever stopped him in the street to say, with gladsome looks, "My dear Scrooge, how are you? When will you come to see me?" No beggars implored him to bestow a trifle, no children asked him what it was o'clock, no man or woman ever once in all his life inquired the way to such and such a place, of Scrooge. Even the blind men's dogs appeared to know him; and when they saw him coming on, would tug their owners into doorways and up courts; and then would wag their tails as though they said, "No eye at all is better than an evil eye, dark master!" But what did Scrooge care!

"Marley was dead"
The only people to register (record) Marley's death and attend his funeral were officials and Scrooge. He must have had no other friends or family.

SCROOGE & MARLEY

The old sign
Marley's death was hardly noticed. Scrooge never even bothered to paint out Marley's name from the sign above the warehouse door.

Grindstone

Grindstone
Grindstones were used to sharpen tools. Scrooge, "a tight-fisted hand at the grindstone", was sharp and mean at work.

"A merry Christmas, uncle! God save you!" cried a cheerful voice.

Counting-house
Business accounts were written down in books called ledgers, which were kept in an office known as a counting-house.

Ledger

Once upon a time – of all the good days in the year, upon Christmas Eve – old Scrooge sat busy in his counting-house. It was cold, bleak, biting, foggy weather, and the city clocks had only just gone three, but it was quite dark already. The door of Scrooge's counting-house was open that he might keep his eye upon his clerk, who in a dismal little cell beyond was copying letters. Scrooge had a very small fire, but the clerk's fire was so very much smaller that it looked like one coal. But he couldn't replenish it, for Scrooge kept the coal-box in his own room; and so surely as the clerk came in with the shovel, the master predicted that it would be necessary for them to part. Wherefore the clerk put on his white comforter, and tried to warm himself at the candle.

"A merry Christmas, uncle! God save you!" cried a cheerful voice. It was the voice of Scrooge's nephew.

"Bah!" said Scrooge, "Humbug!"

"Christmas a humbug, uncle! You don't mean that, I am sure."

"I do," said Scrooge. "Out upon merry Christmas! What's Christmas time to you but a time for paying bills without money; a time for finding yourself a year older, and not an hour richer. Let me leave it alone. Much good may it do you! Much good it has ever done you!"

"I am sure I have always thought of Christmas time," returned the nephew, "as a good time, a kind, forgiving, charitable, pleasant time: the only time I know of, when men and women seem by one consent to open their shut-up hearts freely. And therefore, uncle, though it has never put a scrap of gold or silver in my pocket, I believe that it *has* done me good, and *will* do me good; and I say, God bless it! Come! Dine with us tomorrow."

"Good afternoon," said Scrooge.

"I am sorry, with all my heart, to find you so resolute. A Merry Christmas, uncle!"

"Good afternoon!" said Scrooge.

"And a Happy New Year!"

"Good afternoon!" said Scrooge.

His nephew left the room without an angry word.

Coal
Scrooge's office is as cold as his heart. Scrooge threatens to sack his clerk if he asks for more coal to heat his "little cell".

Ledger

The poor clerk
Dickens had worked as a clerk, and had great sympathy with people in low-paid office jobs. Poor clerks feature in several of his novels. Above is Uriah Heep from David Copperfield.

Quill pen

Ink pot

A clerk's work
Clerks were responsible for the office paperwork. Documents and letters had to be carefully copied by hand. It was repetitive, poorly-paid work.

Comforter

Comforters
A comforter was a woollen scarf. It would not normally be worn indoors, but Scrooge's clerk wore his at work because he was so cold.

People distributing
coal for charity

Christmas charity
*Organized charity at
Christmas grew rapidly in
the 1840s, as did the tradition
of going door-to-door to
collect money.*

Prisons
*Thousands, like Dickens'
father, were imprisoned
because they could not pay
debts. Prison conditions were
terrible. Scrooge's visitors
argue that it is better to give to
the poor than imprison those
guilty of nothing but poverty.*

Visitors at Newgate prison

The clerk, in letting Scrooge's nephew out, had let
two other people in. They had books and papers in
their hands, and bowed to him.

"At this festive season of the year, Mr Scrooge,"
said one of the gentlemen, taking up a
pen, "it is more than usually desirable
that we should make some slight
provision for the poor and destitute,
who suffer greatly at the present time.
Many thousands are in want of
common necessaries; hundreds
of thousands are in want of
common comforts, sir."

"Are there no prisons?"
asked Scrooge.

"Plenty of prisons. But
under the impression that
they scarcely furnish Christian
cheer of mind or body, a few of
us are endeavouring to raise a
fund to buy the poor some meat
and drink, and means of warmth.
We choose this time because it is
a time, of all others, when Want is
keenly felt, and Abundance rejoices.
What shall I put you down for?"

"Nothing!" Scrooge replied.
"I wish to be left alone. I don't
make merry at Christmas and I can't afford to
make idle people merry. I help to support the
prisons and workhouses – they cost enough.
Those who are badly off must go there."

"Many can't go there; and many would
rather die."

"If they would rather die," said Scrooge, "they had better do it."
Seeing clearly that it would be useless to pursue their point,
the gentlemen withdrew.

Foggier yet, and colder! Piercing, searching, biting cold.
The owner of one scant young nose, gnawed by the
hungry cold as bones are gnawed by dogs,
stooped down at Scrooge's keyhole to regale
him with a Christmas carol: but at the
first sound of –

"God bless you merry gentleman!
May nothing you dismay!"

Scrooge seized the ruler with such
energy of action, that the singer
fled in terror, leaving the
keyhole to the fog and frost.
At length the hour of
shutting up the counting-house
arrived. With an ill-will
Scrooge dismounted from his
stool, and admitted the fact to
the expectant clerk, who
instantly snuffed his candle out,
and put on his hat.

"You'll want all day tomorrow,
I suppose?" said Scrooge.

"If quite convenient, sir."

"It's not convenient," said Scrooge, "and
it's not fair. If I was to stop half-a-crown for it,
you'd think yourself ill used, I'll be bound?"

The singer fled in terror,
leaving the keyhole to the
fog and frost.

The clerk smiled faintly and observed that
it was only once a year.

"A poor excuse! But I suppose you must have the whole day. Be
here all the earlier next morning!"

The clerk promised he would; and Scrooge walked out with a growl.

Down-and-outs
on the way to
the workhouse.

Workhouses
Poor people who could not
support themselves had to enter
workhouses. Here they did
harsh jobs for a little food and
a place to sleep.

In Dickens' novel *Oliver Twist*,
Oliver is put in a workhouse.

Poor children
There were
thousands of poor,
often homeless
children on the streets
of London. Singing
carols was a way of
earning a little money.
Scrooge's angry reaction
is completely unfeeling.

Taverns

Usually people went to taverns to drink, relax, and meet other people. Scrooge, however, reads his banker's book to find out how much money he has, and avoids talking to anyone. He then goes to his lonely home. He could have a fine house, surrounded by people, but prefers to live all alone in a commercial building near his work.

Tavern sign

Hearse

Marley's ghostly face has unsettled Scrooge. The gloomy atmosphere of the building, lit only by his cheap "dip", or candle, conjures up the deathly image of a hearse, a vehicle used to carry coffins.

Hearses are black, a colour linked with death and mourning.

Scrooge took his melancholy dinner in his usual melancholy tavern; and having read all the newspapers, and beguiled the rest of the evening with his banker's book, went home to bed. He lived in chambers which had once belonged to his deceased partner. They were a gloomy suite of rooms, in a building that was old enough now, and dreary enough, for nobody lived in it but Scrooge, the other rooms being all let out as offices.

Now, it is a fact, that there was nothing at all particular about the knocker on the door, except that it was very large. Also, that Scrooge had seen it night and morning during his whole residence in that place. And yet Scrooge, having his key in the lock of the door, saw in the knocker, without its undergoing any process of change: not a knocker, but Marley's face.

Marley's face. It was not angry or ferocious, but it looked at Scrooge as Marley used to look: with ghostly spectacles turned up upon its ghostly forehead.

As Scrooge looked fixedly at this phenomenon, it was a knocker again. He said, "Pooh, pooh!" and closed the door with a bang.

The sound resounded through the house like thunder. Every room above, and every cask in the wine-merchant's cellars below, appeared to have a separate peal of echoes of its own. Scrooge was not a man to be frightened by echoes. He fastened the door, and walked across the hall, and up the stairs. Slowly too: trimming his candle as he went.

You might have got a hearse up that staircase. There was plenty of width for that, and room to spare; which is perhaps the reason why Scrooge thought he saw a hearse going on before him in the gloom. Half a dozen gas-lamps out of the street wouldn't have lighted the entry too well, so you may suppose that it was pretty dark with Scrooge's dip.

Up Scrooge went, not caring a button for its being very dark: darkness is cheap, and Scrooge liked it. But before he shut his heavy door, he walked through his rooms to see that all was right.

Sitting-room, bed-room, lumber-room. All as they should be. Nobody under the table, nobody under the sofa and a small fire in

Scrooge, having his key in the lock of the door, saw in the knocker... Marley's face.

the grate. Nobody under the bed; nobody in the closet; nobody in his dressing-gown, which was hanging up in a suspicious attitude against the wall.

Quite satisfied, he closed his door, and locked himself in; double-locked himself in, which was not his custom. Thus secured against surprise, he put on his dressing-gown and slippers, and his nightcap; and sat down before the very low fire.

As he threw his head back in the chair, his glance happened to rest upon a bell, a disused bell, that hung in the room. It was with great astonishment, and with a strange, inexplicable dread, that as he looked, he saw this bell begin to swing. It swung so softly in the outset that it scarcely made a sound; but soon it rang out loudly, and so did every bell in the house.

This might have lasted half a minute, or a minute, but it seemed an hour. The bells ceased as they had begun, together. They were succeeded by a clanking noise, deep down below; as if some person were dragging a heavy chain over the casks in the wine-merchant's cellar. Scrooge then remembered to have heard that ghosts in haunted houses were described as dragging chains.

The silent bells
In rich people's homes, bells were rung to summon servants. Scrooge was too mean to pay for servants, so his bells were "disused".

Cash-box

Marley's ghost is bound and chained by the trappings of a lifetime's dealing with money: cash-boxes, keys, padlocks, ledgers, deeds, and heavy purses.

Then he heard the noise much louder, on the floors below; then coming up the stairs; then coming straight towards his door. It came on through the heavy door, and a spectre passed into the room before his eyes. And upon its coming in, the dying flame leaped up, as though it cried, "*I know him! Marley's ghost!*"

The same face: the very same. Marley in his pigtail, usual waistcoat, tights, and boots. The chain he drew was clasped about his middle. It was long, and wound about him like a tail; and it was made of cash-boxes, keys, padlocks, ledgers, deeds, and heavy purses wrought in steel.

Though he looked the phantom through and through, and saw it standing before him; though he felt the chilling influence of its death-cold eyes; he was still incredulous, and fought against his senses.

"How now!" said Scrooge, cold as ever. "What do you want with me?"

"Much!" – Marley's voice, no doubt about it.

"Who are you?"

"Ask me who I *was*."

"Who *were* you then?" said Scrooge.

"In life I was your partner, Jacob Marley."

"Can you – can you sit down?"

"I can."

"Do it, then."

Scrooge asked the question, because he didn't know whether a ghost might find himself in a condition to take a chair. But the ghost sat down on the opposite side of the fireplace, as if he were quite used to it.

"You don't believe in me," observed the Ghost.

"I don't," said Scrooge.

"What evidence would you have of my reality beyond that of your senses?"

"I don't know," said Scrooge.

"Why do you doubt your senses?"

"Because," said Scrooge, "a little thing affects them. A slight disorder of the stomach makes them cheats. You may be a crumb of cheese, a fragment of an underdone potato. There's more of gravy than of grave about you, whatever you are!"

Scrooge was not much in the habit of cracking jokes, nor did he feel, in his heart, by any means waggish then. The truth is, that he tried to be smart, as a means of keeping down his horror.

How much greater was his horror, when, the phantom taking off the bandage round its head, as if it were too warm to wear indoors, its lower jaw dropped down upon its breast!

Scrooge fell upon his knees, and clasped his hands before his face.

"Mercy!" he said. "Dreadful apparition, why do you trouble me?"

"It is required of every man," the Ghost returned, "that the spirit within him should walk abroad among his fellow men, and travel far and wide; and if that spirit goes not forth in life, it is condemned to do so after death. It is doomed to wander through the world and witness what it cannot share, but might have shared on earth, and turned to happiness."

"You are fettered," said Scrooge, trembling. "Tell me why?"

"I wear the chain I forged in life," replied the Ghost. "I made it link by link, and yard by yard; is its pattern strange to you?"

"I wear the chain I forged in life. I made it link by link, and yard by yard."

"That blessed Star"
This star shone above Jesus' birthplace at the first Christmas, and led the Wise Men to the poor stable. Marley wishes that the Christmas spirit of love had led him to help the poor, while he was still alive to do so.

Unquiet ghosts
Many ghost stories feature characters who are condemned to wander the earth as ghosts after death, for example in the legend of the Flying Dutchman (left and above). Usually such ghosts bring bad luck, but Marley gives Scrooge a chance to change.

"But you were always a good man of business, Jacob," faltered Scrooge, who began to apply this to himself.

"Business!" cried the Ghost. "Mankind was my business. The common welfare was my business; charity, mercy, forbearance, and benevolence, were, all, my business. The dealings of my trade were but a drop of water in the comprehensive ocean of my business! At this time of the rolling year I suffer most. Why did I walk through crowds of fellow-beings with my eyes turned down, and never raise them to that blessed Star which led the Wise Men to a poor abode? Were there no poor homes to which its light would have conducted *me*!"

Scrooge was very much dismayed to hear the spectre going on at this rate, and began to quake exceedingly.

"Hear me!" cried the Ghost. "My time is nearly gone. I am here tonight to warn you, that you have yet a chance and hope of escaping my fate. A chance and hope of my procuring, Ebenezer. You will be haunted by Three Spirits. Expect the first tomorrow night, when the bell tolls one. Expect the second on the next night at the same hour. The third upon the next night when the last stroke of twelve has ceased to vibrate. Look to see me no more; and look that, for your own sake, you remember what has passed between us!"

When it had said these words, the apparition walked backward from him; and at every step it took, the window raised itself a little, so that when the spectre reached it, it was wide open.

Scrooge followed to the window: desperate in his curiosity. He looked out.

*The air was filled with
phantoms, wandering hither
and thither in restless haste,
and moaning as they went.*

The air was filled
with phantoms,
wandering
hither and
thither in
restless
haste, and
moaning
as they
went. Every one of
them wore chains
like Marley's Ghost.

Whether these
creatures faded into mist, or
mist enshrouded them, he could
not tell. But they and their spirit
voices faded together; and the
night became as it had been
when he walked home.

Scrooge closed the window,
went straight to bed, and fell asleep.

"The curtains of his bed"
Wooden four-poster beds with curtains round them were quite common in Scrooge's day.

"Wintry emblem"
Holly is associated with winter and Christmas, but the Spirit also wears summer flowers. In this "singular contradiction" the Spirit combines summer and winter.

"Pedestrian purposes"
Scrooge worries that it was too cold and too late to be walking about outside, as a pedestrian, but the Spirit invites him to fly.

White cotton nightgown

Night-cap

Nightgown and cap
Scrooge, "clad but lightly", was in customary nightwear.

Two

THE FIRST OF THE THREE SPIRITS

WHEN SCROOGE AWOKE, it was so dark, that looking out of bed, he could scarcely distinguish the transparent window from the opaque walls of his chamber until suddenly the church clock tolled a deep, dull, hollow, melancholy ONE. Light flashed up in the room upon the instant, and the curtains of his bed were drawn aside. Scrooge found himself face to face with the unearthly visitor who drew them.

It was a strange figure – like a child: yet not so like a child as like an old man. Its hair, which hung about its neck and down its back, was white as if with age; and yet the face had not a wrinkle in it, and the tenderest bloom was on the skin. The arms, hands, legs and feet were bare. It wore a tunic of the purest white; and round its waist was bound a lustrous belt. It held a branch of fresh green holly in its hand; and, in singular contradiction of that wintry emblem, had its dress trimmed with summer flowers. But the strangest thing about it was, that from the crown of its head there sprung a bright clear jet of light.

"Are you the Spirit, sir, whose coming was foretold to me?" asked Scrooge.

"I am!" The voice was soft and gentle, and low as if instead of being so close beside him, it were at a distance.

"Who, and what are you?" Scrooge demanded.

"I am the Ghost of Christmas Past."

"Long past?" inquired Scrooge.

"No. Your past. The things that you will see with me are Shadows of the things that have been; they will have no consciousness of us. Rise! And walk with me!"

It would have been in vain for Scrooge to plead that the weather and the hour were not adapted to pedestrian purposes; that bed was warm, and the thermometer a long way below freezing; that he was

clad but lightly; and that he had a cold upon him at that time.
The grasp, though gentle as a woman's hand, was not to be resisted.
He rose: but finding that the Spirit made towards the window,
clasped its robe in supplication.

"I am a mortal," Scrooge remonstrated, "and liable to fall."

"Bear but a touch of my hand *there*," said the Spirit, laying it upon
his heart, "and you shall be upheld in more than this!"

*It was a strange figure
– like a child: yet not
so like a child as like
an old man.*

As the words were spoken, they passed through the wall, and stood in the busy thoroughfares of a city. The Ghost stopped at a certain warehouse door, and asked Scrooge if he knew it.

"Know it! Was I apprenticed here?" asked Scrooge.

They went in. At the sight of an old gentleman sitting behind a high desk Scrooge cried: "Why, it's old Fezziwig!" Old Fezziwig laid down his pen, and called out in a comfortable, oily, rich, fat, jovial voice: "Yo ho, there! Ebenezer! No more work tonight. Christmas Eve! Clear away, and let's have lots of room here!"

It was done in a minute. In came

Dances and games
*The Fezziwigs and their guests dance informal old English country dances.
In their game "forfeits", if a player makes a mistake, he has to do whatever the other players tell him to do.*

Arthur Rackham's illustrations of Mrs Fezziwig (above) and Mr Fezziwig (right) from a 1915 edition of *A Christmas Carol*.

Away they all went, twenty couple at once; down the middle and up again.

24

a fiddler with a music-book. In came Mrs Fezziwig, one vast substantial smile. In came the three Miss Fezziwigs, beaming and lovable. In came all the young men and women employed in the business. Away they all went, twenty couple at once; down the middle and up again.

There were more dances, and there were forfeits, and there was cake, and there was a great piece of Cold Roast. But the great effect of the evening came when the fiddler struck up "Sir Roger de Coverley". Then old Fezziwig stood out to dance with Mrs Fezziwig. A positive light appeared to issue from Fezziwig's calves. They shone in every part of the dance.

When the clock struck eleven, this domestic ball broke up. Mr and Mrs Fezziwig took their stations, and shaking hands with every person as he or she went out, wished him or her a Merry Christmas.

"A small matter," said the Ghost, "to make these silly folks so full of gratitude. He has spent but a few pounds of your mortal money."

"It isn't that," said Scrooge, speaking unconsciously like his former, not his latter, self. "He has the power to render us happy or unhappy; to make our service light or burdensome, a pleasure or a toil. The happiness he gives, is quite as great as if it cost a fortune."

A low-life party at Vauxhall Gardens, in London

Respectable dancing
In Scrooge's youth, dancing was perfectly socially acceptable, but by 1843 it was often frowned upon, and linked with low-life places. In this scene, Dickens shows dancing as part of a wholesome, innocent party.

Musicians such as fiddlers played popular dance tunes.

A perfect world
"Sir Roger de Coverley" was a popular dance named after an imaginary ideal country gentleman. Although Fezziwig is a businessman, working in the same commercial world as Scrooge, he acts as a perfect gentleman should, making his apprentice (trainee) Scrooge and the others who work for him happy. As an employer he is the opposite of Scrooge.

Mourning clothes

Black mourning clothes were worn after a loved one died. Scrooge's fiancée wears black to suggest the death of their love and the person he once was.

Mourning jewellery

"Another idol"

The girl says that money has taken her place in Scrooge's heart. Gain has become his "golden" idol, his all-absorbing passion.

An 1840s bride's wedding clothes

No bride for Scrooge

Before he fell in love with money, Scrooge loved his fiancée, who was "dowerless", that is poor, with no money to bring to the marriage. Now she knows that he would resent her poverty.

"My time grows short," observed the Spirit. "Quick!"

This was not addressed to Scrooge, or to anyone whom he could see, but it produced an immediate effect. For again he saw himself. He was older now; a man in the prime of life. His face had not the harsh and rigid lines of later years; but it had begun to wear the signs of care and avarice.

He was not alone, but sat by the side of a fair young girl in a black dress, in whose eyes there were tears.

"It matters little," she said, softly, to Scrooge's former self. "To you, very little. Another idol has displaced me; and if it can comfort you in time to come, as I would have tried to do, I have no just cause to grieve."

"What Idol has displaced you?" he rejoined.

"A golden one. I have seen your nobler aspirations fall off one by one, until the master-passion, Gain, engrosses you."

"What then?" he retorted. "Even if I have grown so much wiser, what then? I am not changed towards you. Have I ever sought release from our engagement?"

"In words. No. Never."

"In what, then?"

"In a changed nature; in an altered spirit; in another atmosphere of life; another Hope as its great end. If you were free today, tomorrow, yesterday, can even I believe that you would choose a dowerless girl: do I not know that your repentance and regret would surely follow? I do; and I release you. With a full heart, for the love of him you once were. May you be happy in the life you have chosen!"

She left him; and they parted.

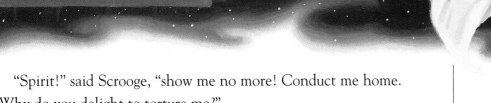

"Spirit!" said Scrooge, "show me no more! Conduct me home. Why do you delight to torture me?"

"One shadow more!" exclaimed the Ghost.

"No more!" cried Scrooge. "No more. I don't wish to see it. Show me no more!"

But the relentless Ghost pinioned him in both his arms, and forced him to observe what happened next.

Scrooge again saw himself … He was not alone, but sat by the side of a fair young girl in a black dress, in whose eyes there were tears.

27

They were in another scene and place: a room, not very large or handsome, but full of comfort. Near to the winter fire sat a beautiful young girl, so like the last that Scrooge believed it was the same, until he saw *her*, now a comely matron, sitting opposite her daughter. The noise in this room was perfectly

The onslaught that was made on the defenceless porter!

tumultuous, for there were more children there than Scrooge in his agitated state of mind could count; and every child was conducting itself like forty. The consequences were uproarious beyond belief; but no one seemed to care; on the contrary, the mother and daughter laughed heartily, and enjoyed it very much; and the latter, soon beginning to mingle in the sports, got pillaged by the young brigands most ruthlessly.

But now a knocking at the door was heard, and a rush immediately ensued towards it, just in time to greet the father, who came home attended by a man laden with Christmas toys and presents. Then the shouting and the struggling, and the onslaught that was made on the defenceless porter! The scaling him with chairs for ladders, to dive into his pockets, despoil him of brown-paper parcels, hold on tight by his cravat, hug him round the neck, pommel his back, and kick his legs in irrepressible affection! The shouts of wonder and delight with which the development of every package was received! The terrible announcement that the

Scrooge's loss
The delighted children show Scrooge how much he has missed: they could have been his.

baby had been taken in the act of putting a doll's frying-pan into his mouth, and was more than suspected of having swallowed a fictitious turkey, glued on a wooden platter! The immense relief of finding this a false alarm! The joy, and gratitude, and ecstasy! They are all indescribable alike. It is enough that by degrees the children and their emotions got out of the parlour and by one stair at a time, up to the top of the house; where they went to bed, and so subsided.

And now Scrooge looked on more attentively than ever, when the master of the house, having his daughter leaning fondly on him, sat down with her and her mother at his own fireside; and when he thought that such another creature, quite as graceful and as full of promise, might have called him father, and been a spring-time in the haggard winter of his life, his sight grew very dim indeed.

"Spirit!" said Scrooge in a broken voice, "remove me from this place."

"I told you these were shadows of the things that have been," said the Ghost. "That they are what they are, do not blame me!"

"Remove me!" Scrooge exclaimed. "I cannot bear it! Leave me! Take me back. Haunt me no longer!"

As he struggled with the Spirit he was conscious of being exhausted, and overcome by an irresistible drowsiness; and further, of being in his own bedroom. He had barely time to reel to bed, before he sank into a heavy sleep.

Toy story
The mass production of toys developed rapidly after 1850. It was spurred on by the developing importance of Christmas celebrations, influenced by this book. Before, toy-making was a cottage industry. Among the presents Dickens was given as a child were a dolls' house, games, and wooden animals.

Victorian dolls, imported from Germany; many toys were imported from continental Europe.

"Happy Families" playing cards

Toys were made of wood, cloth, and often metal, such as tin or lead.

CHRISTMAS IN SCROOGE'S DAY

Christmas decorations

In 1843, Christmas was much less of an event than it is today, and much less commercial. Many people went to church, and many followed the ancient tradition of making merry. Some children received presents. Christmas was seen as a time for being kind to others, although often not much was actually done for those in need. Dickens' visions of Christmas celebrations in *A Christmas Carol* showed people how wonderful Christmas could be, and inspired many to try to help the poor to celebrate, too.

A well-off family opening their food hamper for the Christmas dinner.

THE CHRISTMAS STORY

According to the Christmas Bible story, Christ came down to earth from heaven to be born at Christmas, because of his love for all humanity. So people felt that they should show love for others at Christmas time, to follow his example. Many went to church (above).

Family Christmas

The English Christmas was at a low ebb when Dickens was young. Sometimes national newspapers did not even mention it. There was only one day's holiday, and many people did not get even that. Worse still, for the very poor the holiday made no difference at all; Christmas did not affect their lives. Well-off families, however, would exchange presents, enjoy games and music, and eat special meals, with Christmas pudding and perhaps goose or turkey. Families such as the Cratchits might share games and songs, and a Christmas meal, if they scrimped and saved for it, but could not dream of buying presents.

Fresh fruits

Filberts (hazelnuts)

Mince pies

The "Old Spirit of Christmas", from a magazine of 1843

Toasting glass

Pantomime figure

The "spirit of Christmas"

In 1843, there was an old custom of representing the spirit of Christmas by a jolly figure who brought gifts, food, and drink (right). Dickens borrowed from this tradition when he made the second of the Three Spirits a similar figure. The spirit of Christmas was understood to be a spirit of love, plenty, friendship, comfort, food, and drink.

All the family played games at Christmas.

Christmas holly

OLD TRADITIONS

Many Christmas traditions were very old even in 1843. Some dated from the time of ancient pagan midwinter festivals which were celebrated long before the first Christmas.

Twelfth Night

The old tradition of celebrating Twelfth Night (January 6) as a night of feasting and merriment became part of the Christmas festival, as did the "twelfth-cake", which would often have a lucky bean or coin baked into it. Twelfth Night is still the night when people take down their Christmas decorations in many places.

Twelfth Night celebrations included street musicians.

Christmas carols

These songs about the birth of Christ and the religious meaning of Christmas grew out of a non-religious tradition of singing door-to-door at this time of year. Scrooge drives away the young carol-singer who sings "God bless you merry gentleman" to him, showing how mean he is.

Kissing bough; the apple in the middle represents plenty

Mistletoe, holly, and ivy

In ancient times these evergreens were associated with pagan midwinter celebrations. They were soon incorporated into the Christian Christmas, and by the time A Christmas Carol was written, mistletoe, holly, and ivy were accepted home decorations for everyone. Mistletoe on the "kissing bough" was the centrepiece of a room's decorations.

Christmas trees

The Christmas tree was a long-established tradition in Germany before the 1800s. It became popular in England after the German husband of Queen Victoria made it a part of the royal Christmas. After the 1840s many English families had a tree, if they could afford to. In the USA the custom became widespread from the 1830s, introduced by Germans who moved there.

NEW CHRISTMAS CUSTOMS

In 1843, many of today's favourite Christmas customs had not yet arrived in England. Christmas trees, Christmas cards, Father Christmas (or Santa Claus) – these had not yet become popular parts of the English Christmas. Fifty years later, all of these novelties had become traditions. In other parts of the world, some of them had been popular much earlier.

Christmas gifts

There was nothing like today's commercial extravaganza. Many poor children never saw a Christmas present.

Illustration from an early Christmas card

Christmas cards

The first printed Christmas cards were produced in England in 1843, the year that A Christmas Carol was written.

The children of well-off parents received presents.

Made in America

The figure of Santa Claus arose from stories about Saint Nicholas, a saint popular with Dutch immigrants to America. His modern image was fixed in 1822, by American poet Clement Clarke Moore's poem "The Night before Christmas". He did not become popular in England until the 1870s.

Three

THE SECOND OF THE THREE SPIRITS

SCROOGE AWOKE in his own bedroom. There was no doubt about that. But it, and his own adjoining sitting-room into which he shuffled in his slippers – attracted by a great light there – had undergone a surprising transformation. The walls and ceiling were so hung with living green, that it looked a perfect grove. The crisp leaves of holly, mistletoe, and ivy reflected back the light, as if so many little mirrors had been scattered there; and such a mighty blaze went roaring up the chimney, as that dull hearth had never known in Scrooge's time, or Marley's, or for many and many a winter season gone. Heaped upon the floor, to form a kind of throne, were turkeys, geese, game, brawn, great joints of meat, long wreaths of sausages, mince-pies, plum-puddings, barrels of oysters, red-hot chestnuts, cherry-cheeked apples, juicy oranges, luscious pears, immense twelfth-cakes, and seething bowls of punch. In easy state upon this couch, there sat a jolly Giant, glorious to see; who bore a glowing torch, in shape not unlike Plenty's horn, and who raised it high, to shed its light on Scrooge, as he came peeping round the door.

"Come in!" exclaimed the Ghost. "Come in! And know me better, man!"

Scrooge entered timidly, and hung his head before this Spirit. He was not the dogged Scrooge he had been; and though its eyes were clear and kind, he did not like to meet them.

"I am the Ghost of Christmas Present," said the Spirit. "Look upon me! You have never seen the like of me before!"

"Never. Spirit," said Scrooge submissively, "conduct me where you will. I went forth last night on compulsion, and I learnt a lesson which is working now. Tonight, if you have aught to teach me,

Winter green
Mistletoe, holly, and ivy are evergreen and are therefore used to create an atmosphere of life in the dead of winter.

Holly

Christmas food
The Spirit brings meats, fruit, drinks, and cakes that were special Christmas treats.

Oysters

Punch, made with wine and fruit juice, is still a popular Christmas drink.

Brawn is a kind of preserved, jellied meat.

Plenty's Horn
In ancient Greek legend, the Horn of Plenty gave its owners whatever they desired. Like Plenty's Horn, the Spirit's torch reflects the abundance the Spirit brings with him.

Horn

let me profit by it."

"Touch my robe!"

Scrooge did as he was told, and held it fast.

Holly, mistletoe, red berries, ivy, turkeys, geese, game, poultry, brawn, meat, pigs, sausages, oysters, pies, puddings, fruit, and punch, all vanished instantly. So did the room, the fire, the ruddy glow, the hour of night, and they stood in the city streets on Christmas morning, where (for the weather was severe) the people made a rough, but brisk

In easy state upon this couch, there sat a jolly Giant.

Everything
was good
to eat and in
its Christmas dress.

34

and not unpleasant kind of music, in scraping the snow from the pavement in front of their dwellings. There was nothing very cheerful in the climate or the town, and yet was there an air of cheerfulness abroad.

The poulterers' shops were still half-open, and the fruiterers' were radiant in their glory. There were great, round, pot-bellied baskets of chestnuts, shaped like the waistcoats of jolly old gentlemen. There were pears and apples clustered high in blooming pyramids; there were bunches of grapes, made to dangle from conspicuous hooks, that people's mouths might water as they passed; there were piles of filberts, mossy and brown, recalling, in their fragrance, ancient walks among the woods, and pleasant shufflings ankle deep through withered leaves.

The grocers'! Oh the grocers'! Nearly closed, with perhaps two shutters down, or one; but through those gaps such glimpses! The scales descending on the counter made a merry sound, the blended scents of tea and coffee were so grateful to the nose, the raisins were so plentiful and rare, the almonds so extremely white, the sticks of cinnamon so long and straight, the other spices so delicious, the candied fruits so caked and spotted with molten sugar as to make the coldest lookers-on feel faint.

The figs were moist and pulpy, everything was good to eat and in its Christmas dress: the customers were all so hurried and so eager in the hopeful promise of the day, that they tumbled up against each other at the door, clashing their wicker baskets wildly, and left their purchases upon the counter,

Christmas shopping
This Christmas scene was far away from the reality of most people's Christmases. Only a few could afford the array of treats that Dickens depicts here. He creates an idealized scene, in which everyone is happy, and well-off, to show what Christmas should be like.

Sticks of cinnamon

Candied fruits

Going to church
The bells ringing in the steeples were the signal for Christian Londoners to make their way to their place of worship, whether a large church or a small chapel.

Woollen shawl

Bonnet

Apron Skirt made of thick cotton

"Dressed out but poorly in a twice-turned gown"
Mrs Cratchit's clothes were old and worn, but to make her dress look better and last longer she would turn the cuffs and the collar inside-out.

and came running back to fetch them, and committed hundreds of the like mistakes in the best humour possible.

But soon the steeples called good people all, to church and chapel, and away they came, flocking through the streets in their best clothes, and with their gayest faces.

Scrooge and the Ghost passed on, invisible, straight to Scrooge's clerk's; and on the threshold of the door the Spirit smiled, and stopped to bless Bob Cratchit's dwelling with the sprinkling of his torch.

Then up rose Mrs Cratchit, Cratchit's wife, dressed out but poorly in a twice-turned gown, but brave in ribbons, which are cheap and make a goodly show for sixpence; and she laid the cloth, assisted by Belinda Cratchit, second of her daughters, also brave in ribbons; while Master Peter Cratchit plunged a fork into the saucepan of potatoes.

And now two smaller Cratchits, boy and girl, came tearing in, screaming that, outside the baker's, they had smelt the goose, and known it for their own; and basking in luxurious thoughts of sage and onion, these young Cratchits danced about the table.

"What has ever got your precious father then," said Mrs Cratchit. "And your brother, Tiny Tim; and Martha warn't as late last Christmas Day by half-an-hour!"

"Here's Martha, mother!" said a girl, appearing as she spoke.

"Why, bless your heart alive, my dear, how late you are!" said Mrs Cratchit, kissing her a dozen times, and taking off her shawl and bonnet for her.

"We'd a deal of work to finish up last night," replied the girl, "and had to clear away this morning!"

"Well! Never mind so long as you are come," said Mrs Cratchit. "There's father coming," cried the two young Cratchits, who were everywhere at once. "Hide Martha, hide!"

So Martha hid herself, and in came Bob, the father, with his threadbare clothes darned up and brushed, to look seasonable; and Tiny Tim upon his shoulder. Alas for Tiny Tim, he bore a little crutch, and had his limbs supported by an iron frame!

"Why, where's our Martha?" cried Bob Cratchit, looking round.

"Not coming," said Mrs Cratchit.

"Not coming!" said Bob. "Not coming upon Christmas Day!"

Martha didn't like to see him disappointed, if it were only in joke; so she came out and ran into his arms, while the two young Cratchits hustled Tiny Tim, and bore him off into the wash-house, that he might hear the pudding singing in the copper.

His active little crutch was heard upon the floor, and back came Tiny Tim, escorted by his brother and sister to his stool beside the fire;

On the threshold of the door the Spirit smiled, and stopped to bless Bob Cratchit's dwelling.

Bakery
Many people were not able to cook their Christmas dinners at home, either because they had no oven or because their ovens were not big enough. Bakeries used to open over Christmas and rent out their ovens.

Tiny Tim and his family in the 1970 film *Scrooge*.

Crutch and frame
In Victorian times, some children suffered from diseases that affected their bones and stunted their growth. These were usually caused by a poor diet.

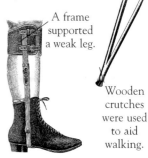

A frame supported a weak leg.

Wooden crutches were used to aid walking.

Family Christmas
This 19th-century painting portrays a poor family, like the Cratchits, sharing Christmas with some visitors.

and while Bob compounded some hot mixture in a jug with gin and lemons, Master Peter and the two young Cratchits went to fetch the goose, with which they soon returned in high procession.

Mrs Cratchit made the gravy hissing hot; Master Peter mashed the potatoes with incredible vigour; Miss Belinda sweetened up the apple-sauce; Martha dusted the hot plates; Bob took Tiny Tim beside him in a tiny corner at the table

Master Peter and the two young Cratchits went to fetch the goose.

and the two young Cratchits set chairs for everybody. At last the dishes were set on, and grace was said. It was succeeded by a breathless pause, as Mrs Cratchit prepared to plunge the carving-knife in the breast; but when she did, and when the long expected gush of stuffing issued forth, one murmur of delight arose all around the board, and even Tiny Tim, excited by the two young Cratchits, beat on the table with the handle of his knife, and feebly cried Hurrah!

There never was such a goose. Its tenderness and flavour, size and cheapness, were the themes of universal admiration. Eked out by the apple-sauce and mashed potatoes, it was a sufficient dinner for the whole family. But now, Mrs Cratchit left the room to take the pudding up, and bring it in. A great deal of steam! The pudding was out of the copper. A smell like a washing-day! That was the cloth. A smell like an eating-house, and a pastry cook's next door to each other, with a laundress's next door to that! That was the pudding. In half a minute Mrs Cratchit entered – flushed, but smiling proudly – with the pudding, like a speckled cannon-ball, so hard and firm, blazing in half of half-a-quartern of ignited brandy, and bedight with Christmas holly stuck into the top.

Oh, a wonderful pudding! Bob Cratchit said that he regarded it as the greatest success achieved by Mrs Cratchit since their marriage. Everybody had something to say about it, but nobody said or thought it was at all a small pudding for a large family.

Goose

A goose was the Christmas food of poorer working people. Turkeys were preferred by richer folk, and very many people could not afford any kind of special meal. Goose clubs became popular: people paid in for several months for the chance to win a goose in a raffle.

Goose cooked with stuffed apples

Mashed potato

Apple sauce

Christmas pudding

The Christmas pudding, or plum pudding, was originally made with a little meat, spices, dried fruit, flour, and breadcrumbs. It was wrapped in a cloth and boiled for many hours in a "copper", a large container normally used for the household washing.

Christmas pudding is still a popular Christmas dish today.

A poor roadsweeper buying chestnuts from a street seller.

Chestnuts

Chestnuts were a traditional Christmas treat, roasted in their shells on an open fire. At other times, they were often bought from street sellers.

Chestnuts

Toast

When people toast someone, or "drink their health", they raise their glasses, and then all drink together in honour of that person or thing. It is a mark of Bob's generous spirit, that he should wish to toast Scrooge.

At last the dinner was all done, the cloth was cleared and the fire made up. Then all the Cratchit family drew round the hearth and Bob proposed:

"A Merry Christmas to us all, my dears. God bless us!"

Which all the family re-echoed.

"God bless us every one!" said Tiny Tim, the last of all. He sat very close to his father's side, upon his little stool. Bob held his withered little hand in his, as if he loved the child, and wished to keep him by his side, and dreaded that he might be taken from him.

"Spirit," said Scrooge, "tell me if Tiny Tim will live."

"I see a vacant seat, " replied the Ghost, "in the poor chimney corner, and a crutch without an owner. If these shadows remain unaltered by the Future, the child will die."

Scrooge cast his eyes upon the ground. But he raised them speedily, on hearing his own name. "Mr Scrooge!" said Bob; "I'll give you Mr Scrooge, the Founder of the Feast!"

"The Founder of the Feast indeed!" cried Mrs Cratchit, reddening. "It should be Christmas Day, I am sure, on which one drinks the health of such an odious, stingy, hard, unfeeling man as Mr Scrooge. I'll drink his health for your sake and the Day's, not for his!"

The mention of Scrooge's name cast a dark shadow on the party, which was not dispelled for full five minutes. After it had passed away, Bob Cratchit told them how he had a situation in his eye for Master Peter, which would bring in full five-and-sixpence weekly. Martha, who was a poor apprentice at a milliner's, then told them what kind of work she had to do, and how many hours she worked at a stretch. All this time the chestnuts and the jug went round and round; and bye and bye they had a song from Tiny Tim.

There was nothing of high mark in this. They were not a handsome family; they were not well dressed; their shoes were far from being waterproof; their clothes were scanty; and Peter might have known, and very likely did, the inside of a pawnbroker's. But they were happy, grateful, pleased with one another, and contented with the time; and when they faded, and looked happier yet in the bright sprinklings of the Spirit's torch at parting, Scrooge had his eye upon them, and especially on Tiny Tim, until the last.

"A Merry Christmas to us all, my dears. God bless us!"

"A situation"
By "a situation", Bob means a job. "Five-and-sixpence" is a tiny salary, only a third of Bob's own meagre wage, but to young Peter Cratchit it seems a fortune.

Milliners' job
Milliners made hats, and were usually women or girls. Since almost everyone wore a hat in the 1840s, there was lots of work for milliners, but pay was low and hours long.

Silk bonnet

Pawnbroker's sign

Pawnbroker
Poor people raised money by selling valuables to a pawnbroker. The goods could be bought back within a certain time.

People queueing outside a pawnbroker's shop.

Upon a dismal reef of sunken rocks … there stood a solitary lighthouse.

A solitary place
Lighthouses are among the loneliest places on earth. The Spirit of Christmas can touch this solitary rock, but could not touch Scrooge's lonely heart for many years, until now.

The Spirit bade Scrooge hold his robe, and passing on, sped whither? To sea. To Scrooge's horror, looking back, he saw the last of the land, a frightful range of rocks, behind them; and his ears were deafened by the thundering of water, as it rolled, and roared, and raged among the dreadful caverns it had worn, and fiercely tried to undermine the earth.

Built upon a dismal reef of sunken rocks, some league or so from shore, on which the waters chafed and dashed, the wild year through, there stood a solitary lighthouse. Great heaps of seaweed clung to its base, and storm-birds – born of the wind one might suppose, as seaweed of the water – rose and fell about it, like the waves they skimmed.

But even here, two men who watched the light had made a fire, that through the loophole in the thick stone wall shed out a ray of brightness on the awful sea. Joining their horny hands over the rough table at which they sat, they wished each other Merry Christmas; and one of them, the elder, too, with his face all damaged and scarred with hard weather, struck up a sturdy song that was like a gale in itself.

Again the Ghost sped on, above the black and heaving sea – on, on – until, being far away, as he told Scrooge, from any shore, they lighted on a ship. They stood beside the helmsman at the wheel, the look-out in the bow, the officers who had the watch; dark, ghostly figures

The lighthouse men
The lighthouse men are far from home, family, church, or any visible reminder of Christmas. Yet the day is still a celebration for them.

The ship at sea
Even the sailors at their work, at the bow (front) of the ship, or on "the watch" (in charge of the ship), remember Christmas.

in their several stations; but every
man among them hummed a Christmas
tune, or had a Christmas thought, or spoke below
his breath to his companion of some bygone Christmas
Day, with homeward hopes belonging to it. And every
man on board, waking or sleeping, good or bad, had had a
kinder word for another on that day than on any day in the
year; and had shared to some extent in its festivities; and had
remembered those he cared for at a distance, and had known that
they delighted to remember him.

It was a great surprise to Scrooge, while listening to the moaning of
the wind, and thinking what a solemn thing it was to move on through
the lonely darkness, to hear a hearty laugh. It was a much greater
surprise to Scrooge to recognize it as his own nephew's, and to find
himself in a bright, dry, gleaming room, with the Spirit standing smiling
by his side!

"Ha, ha!" laughed Scrooge's nephew. When Scrooge's nephew
laughed, Scrooge's niece, by marriage, laughed as heartily as he. And
their assembled friends, not a bit behind-hand, laughed out, lustily.

"He said that Christmas was a humbug, as I live!" cried Scrooge's
nephew. "He believed it too!"

"More shame for him, Fred!" said Scrooge's niece indignantly.

"He's a comical old fellow," said Scrooge's nephew, "that's the
truth; and not so pleasant as he might be. However, his
offences carry their own punishment, and I have
nothing to say against him. Who suffers by his
ill whims? Himself, always. Here, he takes it
into his head to dislike us, and he won't
come and dine with us. What's the
consequence?"

"Indeed, I think he loses a very
good dinner," interrupted
Scrooge's niece. Everybody
else said the same,
and they

44

must be allowed to
have been competent judges, because they had just
had dinner; and, with the dessert upon the table,
were clustered round the fire, by lamplight.

"I was going to say," said Scrooge's nephew, "that
the consequence of his taking a dislike to us is that he
loses some pleasant moments. He may rail at Christmas till
he dies, but if he finds me going there, in good temper, year after
year, and saying Uncle Scrooge, how are you? If it only puts him
in the vein to leave his poor clerk fifty pounds, that's something."

It was a great surprise to Scrooge
... to hear a hearty laugh.

Blind-man's buff can be played by adults, or children, or both together.

Blind-man's buff

In blind-man's buff one person is blindfolded and has to chase the rest. Dickens says that it is good for adults to play, as children do, and not to take themselves too seriously. The "mighty Founder" is Jesus Christ.

Lace tucker, very fashionable in the 1840s

Lace tucker

The first person to be blindfolded is Scrooge's nephew's friend Topper. The plump sister, of whom he is fond, wears a "lace tucker", a little piece of lace worn above a low-cut dress.

After a while they played at forfeits; for it is good to be children sometimes, and never better than at Christmas, when its mighty Founder was a child himself. There was a game of blind-man's buff. Of course there was. And I no more believe Topper was really blinded than I believe he had eyes in his boots. Because, the way in which he went after that plump sister in the lace tucker, was an outrage. Knocking down the fire irons, tumbling over the chairs, bumping against the piano, smothering himself among the curtains, wherever she went, there went he.

Scrooge had imperceptibly become gay and light of heart. But the scene passed off; and he and the Spirit were again upon their travels.

Much they saw, and far they went, and many homes they visited, but always with a happy end. The Spirit stood beside sick beds, and they were cheerful; on foreign lands, and they were close at home; by struggling men, and they were patient in their greater hope; by poverty, and it was rich. In almshouse, hospital, and jail, in misery's every refuge, where man had not barred the Spirit out, he left his blessing, and taught Scrooge his precepts.

"Forgive me," said Scrooge, as they stood together in an open place, "but I see something strange, protruding from your skirts. Is it a foot or a claw!"

From the foldings of its robe, the Spirit brought two children; wretched, abject, frightful, hideous, miserable. They knelt down at its feet, and clung upon the outside of its

garment. They were a boy and girl.

Scrooge started back, appalled.

"Spirit! Are they yours?" Scrooge could say no more.

"They are Man's," said the Spirit. "This boy is Ignorance. This girl is Want. Beware them both, but most of all beware of this boy, for on his brow I see that written which is Doom, unless the writing be erased."

"Have they no refuge or resource?" cried Scrooge.

"Are there no prisons?" said the Spirit, turning on him with his own words. "Are there no workhouses?"

The bell struck *Twelve*.

Scrooge looked about him for the Ghost, and saw it no more. As the last stroke ceased to vibrate, he remembered the prediction of old Jacob Marley, and beheld a solemn Phantom, draped and hooded, coming, like a mist along the ground, towards him.

Fire irons
Fire irons

In their excitement, the young people knocked down the fire irons. These were the poker, tongs, and other tools used for tending the fire.

Almshouse
Almshouses were homes maintained by charities for the poor. The Spirit visits and blesses all the poorest and most unfortunate people.

Ignorance and Want
The two children are symbols of the ignorance and want that dominated the poor areas of cities. Dickens believed that lack of education, and the oppression and misery that went with it, would eventually cause the poor to riot and revolt, unless something was done about it.

There was a game of blind-man's buff.

Four

THE LAST OF THE SPIRITS

THE PHANTOM SLOWLY, gravely, silently, approached. When it came near him, Scrooge bent down upon his knee; for in the very air through which this Spirit moved it seemed to scatter gloom and mystery.

It was shrouded in a deep black garment, which concealed its head, its face, its form, and left nothing of it visible save one outstretched hand. But for this it would have been difficult to detach its figure from the night, and separate it from the darkness by which it was surrounded.

He felt that it was tall and stately when it came beside him, and that its mysterious presence filled him with solemn dread. He knew no more, for the Spirit neither spoke nor moved.

"I am in the presence of the Ghost of Christmas Yet To Come?" said Scrooge. "Ghost of the Future! I fear you more than any Spectre I have seen. But as I know your purpose is to do me good, and as I hope to live to be another man from what I was, I am prepared to bear you company, and do it with a thankful heart. Will you not speak to me?"

It gave him no reply. The hand was pointed straight before them.

"Lead on!" said Scrooge. "Lead on! The night is waning fast, and it is precious time to me, I know. Lead on, Spirit!"

Scrooge bent down upon his knee ... this Spirit seemed to scatter gloom and mystery.

They scarcely seemed to enter the city; for the city rather seemed to spring up about them. But there they were, in the heart of it, amongst the merchants.

The Spirit stopped beside one little knot of business men. Observing that the hand was pointed to them, Scrooge advanced to listen to their talk.

"No," said a great fat man with a monstrous chin, "I don't know much about it, either way. I only know he's dead."

"When did he die?" inquired another.

"Last night, I believe."

"Why, what was the matter with him?" asked a third. "I thought he'd never die."

"God knows," said the first, with a yawn.

"What has he done with his money?" asked a red-faced gentleman.

"I haven't heard," said the man with the large chin, yawning again. "Left it to his Company, perhaps. He hasn't left it to *me*. That's all I know. Bye, bye!"

Scrooge was at first inclined to be surprised that the Spirit should attach importance to conversation apparently so trivial; but feeling assured that it must have some hidden purpose, he set himself to consider what it was likely to be. It could scarcely be supposed to have any bearing on the death of Jacob, his old partner, for that was Past, and this Ghost's province was the Future.

He looked about in that very place for his own image; but another man stood in his accustomed corner, and though the clock pointed to his usual time of day for being there, he saw no likeness of himself among the multitudes that poured in. It gave him little surprise, however; for he had been revolving in his mind a change of life, and he thought and hoped he saw his new-born resolutions carried out in this.

A pale light, rising in the outer air, fell straight upon the bed.

The shop
This is a "rag and bone" shop where old bits and pieces and rubbish, including rags and bones, were bought and sold. As the dead man's possessions have ended up here, it means there are no relatives to inherit them or sort them out.

Arthur Rackham's picture of the rag and bone shop, from a 1915 edition of *A Christmas Carol*.

They left the busy scene, and went into an obscure part of the town, to a shop where iron, old rags, bottles, bones and greasy offal were bought by a grey-haired rascal.

Scrooge and the Phantom came into the presence of this man, just as a woman with a heavy bundle slunk into the shop. But she had scarcely entered, when another woman, similarly laden, came in too; and she was closely followed by a man in faded black.

"Let the charwoman be the first!" cried she who had entered first. "Let the laundress be the second; and let the undertaker's man be the third."

"What have you got to sell?" asked Joe.

"Half a minute's patience, Joe, and you shall see. Who's the worse for the loss of a few things like these? Not a dead man, I suppose. If he wanted to keep 'em after he was dead," pursued the woman, "why wasn't he natural in his lifetime? If he had been, he'd have had somebody to look after him when he was struck with Death, instead of lying gasping out his last there alone by himself. Open that bundle, old Joe, and let me know the value of it. Speak out plain."

Joe went down on his knees, and having unfastened a great many knots, dragged out a large and heavy roll of some dark stuff.

"What do you call this?" said Joe. "Bed-curtains!"

"Ah!" returned the woman. "Bed-curtains! Don't drop that oil upon the blankets, now."

"*His* blankets?" asked Joe.

"Whose else's do you think?" replied the woman. "He isn't likely to take cold without 'em, I dare say. Ah! You may look through that shirt till your eyes ache; but you won't find a hole in it, nor a threadbare place. It's the best he had, and a fine one too."

Scrooge listened to this dialogue with horror.

"Spirit!" said Scrooge. "The case of this unhappy man might be my own. My life tends that way, now. Merciful Heaven, what is this!"

The scene had changed, and now he almost touched a bare, uncurtained bed. A pale light, rising in the outer air, fell straight upon the bed; and on it, unwatched, unwept, uncared for, was the body of this plundered man unknown.

None to mourn him
If the dead man had been "natural" (shown common kindness), there would have been someone to mourn him and look after his affairs when he died. In Victorian times mourning was very important.

Laundresses washing and drying clothes.

Working women
The charwoman and the laundress would have had the opportunity to take some of the dead man's things from his house when they came to clean up and wash his clothes.

Undertaker's man
The undertaker's assistant would help to prepare the body for burial. A dishonest assistant would be able to sell off some of the dead person's possessions.

"And He took a child …"
Peter's book is the Bible. In this passage (Mark 9:36) "He" refers to Jesus, who has a special love for children like Tiny Tim.

Family mourning a dead child

"The colour hurts my eyes"
Mrs Cratchit is crying for Tiny Tim, who has died. She wishes to hide her tears from the children, so she pretends her eyes are watering because of sewing in bad light.

Tea on hob
The hob was the shelf by the fire, where the kettle was kept hot. Mrs Cratchit and the Cratchit children, in their own grief, take extra care of Bob.

Graveyard
The "green place" is the graveyard where Tiny Tim is buried. In death, he is surrounded by life and growth.

"Spirit! Let me see some tenderness connected with a death, or this dark chamber, Spirit, will be for ever present to me," said Scrooge.

The Ghost conducted him to poor Bob Cratchit's house; and found the mother and the children seated round the fire.

Quiet. Very quiet. The noisy little Cratchits were as still as statues, and sat looking up at Peter, who had a book before him.

"'And He took a child, and set him in the midst of them.'"
Where had Scrooge heard those words? He had not dreamed them. The boy must have read them out, as he and the Spirit crossed the threshold. Why did he not go on?

The mother laid her sewing upon the table, and put her hand up to her face.

"The colour hurts my eyes," she said.

The colour? Ah, poor Tiny Tim!

"They're better now again," said Cratchit's wife. "It makes them weak by candle-light; and I wouldn't show weak eyes to your father when he comes home, for the world. It must be near his time."

"Past it rather," Peter answered, shutting up his book. "But I think he's walked a little slower than he used, these last few evenings, mother."

"I have known him walk with – I have known him walk with Tiny Tim upon his shoulder, very fast indeed. But he was very light to carry," she resumed, intent upon her work, "and his father loved him so, that it was no trouble – no trouble. And there is your father at the door!"

She hurried out to meet him; and little Bob in his comforter – he had need of it, poor fellow – came in. His tea was ready for him on the hob. The two young Cratchits got upon his knees and laid, each child a little cheek, against his face, as if they said, "Don't mind it, father. Don't be grieved!"

Bob was very cheerful with them, and spoke pleasantly to all the family.

"You went today then, Robert?" said his wife.

"Yes, my dear," returned Bob. "I wish you could

have gone. It would have done you good to see how green a place it is. I promised him that I would walk there on a Sunday. My little, little child!" cried Bob. "My little child!"

He broke down all at once. He couldn't help it.

He broke down all at once. He couldn't help it.

"Ruinous churchyard"
In death, Scrooge is unloved and uncared for, unlike Tiny Tim. His grave is neglected. No one visits it, and no one remembers him.

"Spectre," said Scrooge, "something informs me that our parting moment is at hand. I know it, but I know not how. Tell me what man that was whom we saw lying dead?"

The Ghost of Christmas Yet To Come conveyed him to a dismal, wretched, ruinous churchyard.

The Spirit stood among the graves, and pointed down to One.

The end?
When Scrooge says "Men's courses will foreshadow certain ends" he means that people's actions lead to particular results. If Scrooge can change his ways, he may change his future.

"I am not the man I was"
Scrooge cries out that he has changed because of what the three spirits have shown him. He hopes that he can change the future by living a better "altered life".

"Before I draw nearer to that stone to which you point," said Scrooge, "answer me one question. Are these the shadows of the things that Will be, or are they shadows of things that May be, only?"

Still the Ghost pointed downward to the grave by which it stood.

"Men's courses will foreshadow certain ends, to which, if persevered in, they must lead," said Scrooge. "But if the courses be departed from; the ends will change. Say it is thus with what you show me!"

The Spirit was as immovable as ever. Scrooge crept towards it, trembling as he went; and following the finger, read upon the stone of the neglected grave his own name, EBENEZER SCROOGE.

"Am I that man who lay upon the bed?" he cried, upon his knees. "No, Spirit! Oh no, no Spirit, hear me! I am not the man I was. I will not be the man I must have been but for this. Why show me this, if I am past all hope? Assure me that I yet may change these shadows you

The Spirit stood among the graves, and pointed down to One.

have shown me, by an altered life."

For the first time, the kind hand faltered.

"I will honour Christmas in my heart, and try to keep it all the year. I will live in the Past, the Present, and the Future. The Spirits of all Three shall strive within me. I will not shut out the lessons that they teach. Oh, tell me I may sponge away the writing on this stone!"

Holding up his hands in one last prayer to have his fate reversed, he saw an alteration in the Phantom's hood and dress. It shrunk, collapsed, and dwindled down into a bedpost.

"Live in the Past, Present, and Future"
By this Scrooge means that he will always keep the three spirits and their lessons in his mind, "all the year" round. It is a promise that he will live a changed and better life.

55

Five

THE END OF IT

YES! and the bedpost was his own. The bed was his own, the room was his own. Best and happiest of all, the time before him was his own, to make amends in! Running to the window he opened it, and put out his head. No fog, no mist, no night; clear, bright, stirring, golden Day.

"What's today?" cried Scrooge, calling downward to a boy in Sunday clothes, who perhaps had loitered in to look about him.

"Eh?"

"What's today, my fine fellow?" said Scrooge.

"Today! Why, CHRISTMAS DAY."

"It's Christmas Day!" said Scrooge to himself. "I haven't missed it. Hallo, my fine fellow! Do you know the Poulterer's, in the next street but one, at the corner?" Scrooge inquired.

"I should hope I did," replied the lad.

"An intelligent boy!" said Scrooge. "A remarkable boy! Do you know whether they've sold the prize Turkey that was hanging up there? Not the little prize Turkey, the big one?"

"What, the one as big as me?"

"A delightful boy! It's a pleasure to talk to him. Yes!"

"It's hanging there now," replied the boy.

"Is it?" said Scrooge. "Go and buy it, and tell 'em to bring it here, that I may give them the direction where to take it. Come back with the man, and I'll give you a shilling. Come back with him in less than five minutes, and I'll give you half-a-crown!"

The boy was off like a shot.

"I'll send it to Bob Cratchit's!" whispered Scrooge. "He shan't know who sends it. It's twice

"What's today, my fine fellow?" said Scrooge.

56

the size of Tiny Tim."

The hand in which he wrote the address was not a steady one, but write it he did, somehow, and went downstairs to open the street door, ready for the coming of the poulterer's man. It *was* a Turkey! He never could have stood upon his legs, that bird. He would have snapped 'em short off in a minute, like sticks of sealing-wax.

Scrooge dressed himself, and at last got out into the streets. The people were by this time pouring forth. Walking with his hands behind him, Scrooge regarded everyone with a delighted smile.

In the afternoon, he turned his steps towards his nephew's house.

He passed the door a dozen times, before he had the courage to go up and knock. But he made a dash, and did it.

"Is your master at home, my dear?" said Scrooge to the girl.

"Yes, sir."

"Where is he, my love?" said Scrooge.

"He's in the dining-room, sir, along with mistress."

"He knows me," said Scrooge, with his hand already on the dining-room lock. "I'll go in here, my dear. Fred!"

"Why bless my soul!" cried Fred, "who's that?"

"It's I. Your uncle Scrooge. I have come to dinner. Will you let me in, Fred?"

Let him in! It is a mercy he didn't shake his arm off. He was at home in five minutes. Nothing could be heartier. His niece looked just the same. So did Topper when he came. So did the plump sister, when she came. Wonderful party, wonderful games, wonderful unanimity, won-der-ful happiness!

But he was early at the office next morning. Oh, he was early there. If he could only be there first, and catch Bob Cratchit coming late! That was the thing he had set his heart upon.

And he did it. The clock struck nine. No Bob. A quarter past. No Bob. Bob was full eighteen minutes and a half, behind his time.

Bob's hat was off, before he opened the door; his comforter too. He was on his stool in a jiffy; driving away with his pen, as if he were trying to overtake nine o'clock.

"Hallo!" growled Scrooge, in his accustomed voice as near as he could feign it.

A poulterer's shop sold turkeys, chickens, and other birds.

Christmas giver
Now Scrooge is being kind to the Cratchits, to the boy in the street, and to his nephew's maid; poor people for whom he wouldn't have had a kind thought or a good word in the past.

Extravagant Scrooge
A shilling would have been a big tip. A half-crown (two and a half shillings) was an enormous tip, nearly half of Peter Cratchit's hoped-for weekly wage.

Pennies: 12 pennies made one shilling.

Stick of sealing-wax

"Sticks of sealing-wax"
These were thin, brittle pieces of wax that were melted and dripped onto an envelope to seal it up. Scrooge's gift to the Cratchits is far too big to stand on normal turkey legs!

"We will discuss your affairs this very afternoon, over a Christmas bowl of smoking bishop!"

Warm fire
Scrooge shares his Christmas cheer by offering Bob a drink of "smoking bishop" (a type of warm punch). Before, he wouldn't let Bob have more coal, now he tells him to buy a coal-scuttle for his room.

The old Scrooge

A new man
Scrooge seems so different that Bob is at first taken aback; but Scrooge really is a changed man, and looks at the world afresh, with love and laughter.

"What do you mean by coming here at this time of day?"

"I am very sorry, sir. I am behind my time."

"You are?" repeated Scrooge. "Yes. I think you are. Step this way, if you please."

"It's only once a year, sir," pleaded Bob. "It shall not be repeated. I was making rather merry yesterday, sir."

"Now, I'll tell you what, my friend, I am not going to stand this sort of thing any longer. And therefore," Scrooge continued, "I am about to raise your salary!"

Bob trembled, and had a momentary idea of calling to the people in the court for help.

"A merry Christmas, Bob!" said Scrooge, with an earnestness that could not be mistaken, as he clapped him on the back. "A merrier Christmas, Bob, my good fellow, than I have given you, for many a year! I'll raise your salary, and endeavour to assist your struggling family, and we will discuss your affairs this very afternoon, over a Christmas bowl of smoking bishop! Make up the fires, and buy another coal-scuttle before you dot another i, Bob Cratchit!"

Scrooge was better than his word. He did it all, and infinitely more; and to Tiny Tim, who did NOT die, he was a second father. He became as good a friend, as good a master, and as good a man, as the good old city knew, or any other good old city, town, or borough, in the good old world. Some people laughed to see the alteration in him, but his own heart laughed: and that was quite enough for him.

He had no further intercourse with Spirits; and it was always said of him, that he knew how to keep Christmas well, if any man alive possessed the knowledge. May that be truly said of us, and all of us! And so, as Tiny Tim observed, God bless Us, Every One!

*He became as good a
friend, as good a
master, and as good a
man, as the good old
city knew.*

CHARLES DICKENS

Charles Dickens' signature

Dickens was one of the greatest of all English writers, and *A Christmas Carol* shows his writing at its best. His books combine humour, unforgettable characters, dramatic stories, anger against injustice and suffering, and a fierce compassion for the poor. In all of them, he spoke out against the Scrooges of the world, and for the Cratchits, the downtrodden people he saw around him. He used his books to show his readers the dark side of their country, and inspired them to change it for the better. He was immensely popular, and had a great influence for good on British society.

DICKENS' LIFE

Charles Dickens was born in Portsmouth, in 1812. When he was 10, his family moved to London, the city which was his great inspiration. His family experienced great poverty, so he lost the chance of a good education, but he read widely.

Dickens' childhood
When Dickens was 12, his father was sent to prison for debt. Charles had to work in a filthy factory, and was haunted by the memory for the rest of his life. He later worked as a solicitor's clerk, doing the same sort of work as Bob Cratchit.

An artist's impression of Dickens working in the factory

Fame comes swiftly
Dickens began to have stories published in magazines in 1833.

He was married in 1836, and in the same year he started *The Pickwick Papers*, a serialized novel completed in 1837. It was a huge success and he was suddenly very famous.

Dickens in 1842

Dickens' wife, Catherine

The living legend
In the next seven years, Dickens wrote five more enormously successful novels. For the rest of his life he was probably the world's most famous living writer. When he died, thousands queued to file past his coffin. Across the Atlantic, the American poet Longfellow noted: "This whole country is stricken with grief."

Dickens in 1869

Dickens and charities
Dickens' childhood poverty, and his many wanderings through the poorer parts of London, had showed him the immense misery and suffering that scarred Britain. He made speeches, wrote articles, and used his novels to fight these evils, and to support schools for poor children, education for adult working people, better sanitation and public health in London, and many other causes.

A view of London in 1823, when Dickens was a boy

Public readings
Dickens' first public reading was of *A Christmas Carol*, to raise funds for a new Industrial and Literary Institute, in Birmingham. He wanted poor people to be admitted free, or at least very cheaply. He also gave a number of readings of this book to raise funds for the Hospital for Sick Children at Great Ormond Street in London.

One of London's thousands of poor children receiving a charitable gift of food

The Hospital for Sick Children, Great Ormond Street, London

Readings for money
Dickens' charitable readings were so successful that he began doing commercial readings, travelling around Britain and the USA, to enormous acclaim. He read from a number of his books, but *A Christmas Carol* was the favourite.

Dickens' readings proved him a natural actor.

Unforgettable energy

Dickens was such a forceful personality that no one who met him ever forgot him, and he had amazing energy. He had ten children, edited his own magazines, travelled widely, wrote thousands of letters, produced and acted in plays, and was writing his 15th novel when he died in 1870.

Dickens' dream, an unfinished painting by R. W. Buss

DICKENS' CHARACTERS

Dickens filled his books with a whole universe full of memorable characters, drawn from every part of the British society of his time. Some, like Scrooge, are far larger than life, and have become legends.

David Copperfield and Mr Micawber from David Copperfield

He broke new ground by making many of his most important characters children or poor people.

Mrs Gamp from *Martin Chuzzlewit*

Children to the fore

Dickens featured children more than any novelist before him, in novels such as *David Copperfield* and *Oliver Twist*.

Fagin from Oliver Twist

Real villains

Dickens' villains are often very, very bad, but they are drawn with such energy that they are more fascinating than repulsive.

Immortal eccentrics

Eccentric Dickens characters like Scrooge and Mrs Gamp illuminate aspects of human nature by exaggerating them.

Sam Weller from The Pickwick Papers

Hard-up heroes

Dickens' heroes are not superhuman. They are ordinary people who triumph over, or at least survive, great troubles.

Little Dorrit from Little Dorrit

A world of women

Dickens created a very wide range of female characters. One of the best-loved of them all is the innocent and good Little Dorrit.

Dickens on screen

Dickens' novels and stories have been made into many films and television series, seen all around the world. These have made him famous among people who have never read his books.

A scene from the BBC's Martin Chuzzlewit *(1994)*

A TV version of Little Dorrit *(1987)*

This painting shows Dickens in the study of his house at Gad's Hill Place in Kent.

A CHRISTMAS CAROL

As soon as it was published, *A Christmas Carol* was acclaimed as a classic, first in Britain, then around the world. It gave people, for the first time, a picture of an ideal Christmas in a city setting, inspiring them to make Christmas better for the poor. It has been retold in many different ways, adapted for radio and television, and made into films, plays, musicals, and even operas. When people talk of the spirit of Christmas, they think of *A Christmas Carol*.

A 1915 picture of Scrooge by Arthur Rackham

The Ghost of Christmas Past

The origins of the story

A Christmas Carol echoes a story told in Dickens' first novel, *The Pickwick Papers*. Here, a grumpy old man, Gabriel Grub, is converted to goodness overnight by friendly goblins, who show him a vision of the Christmas shared by a poor family.

A Christmas scene from The Pickwick Papers

The writing of the book

Dickens wrote the story in just six weeks, in October and November 1843. As he wrote, it "seized him" with "a strange mastery": he wept over it, laughed, wept again, and took long night walks through London as he thought it through. It was an instant success: rushed out in time for Christmas, it had to be reprinted before New Year.

An illustration by John Leech from the first edition

The Ghost of Christmas Present

Friendly ghosts

In most ghost stories the ghosts bring bad luck. In this one they come to teach Scrooge the truth about his life. The first ghost shows him what he has missed out on in the past. The second shows him the fun, family affection, and friendship that he could be sharing. The third reveals the fate that awaits him unless he changes. In a single night, they convert him from selfishness and sadness to goodness and joy.

GHOST STORIES

A Christmas Carol contains visual images and predictions of the future that draw on, and freely adapt, a tradition of ghostly and supernatural tales. Stories of the supernatural were very popular at this time. For example, Edgar Allan Poe's story The Telltale Heart *was also published in 1843.*

Different approaches

Dickens includes such regular ghost story features as a graveyard scene, but his ghosts are far from the sinister figures of most ghostly tales.

A mid-19th-century painting of a ghostly figure

An illustration by Harry Clarke from The Telltale Heart

The Ghost of Christmas Yet To Come

THE LEGACY

After 1843, as the impact of A Christmas Carol spread, Christmas charities boomed. Its influence for good has been immense. To give just one example, an American factory owner who heard Dickens read the story decided to give his workers Christmas Day off, for the first time ever, and gave each of them a turkey for Christmas every year thereafter.

Great illustrators have loved A Christmas Carol; here is Arthur Rackham's picture of Scrooge visiting his nephew.

Bob and Tiny Tim, drawn by Fred Barnaud

Marley's ghost

Marley's ghost is very much a traditional ghostly figure, condemned to walk the earth, complete with chains. But he, too, wishes only Scrooge's good.

Sir Alec Guinness as Marley in A Christmas Carol

STAGE AND SCREEN

The year after it was published, nine London theatres staged versions of this book, and it has been a favourite of stage and screen ever since. Perhaps the classic film was the 1951 version. Some versions have changed the story completely: in Scrooged (1988), Scrooge is the president of a television company.

A poster for the 1970 film musical version

Seymour Hicks as Scrooge in the serious and convincing 1935 film, Scrooge

Alistair Sim plays Scrooge in the 1951 film version

Christmas stories

After the success of A Christmas Carol, Dickens wrote a Christmas story each year for the next few years, including The Chimes (1844) and The Cricket on the Hearth (1845). But none of his other Christmas stories were as popular as A Christmas Carol. It has even added a word to the English language – "a Scrooge" is a miser – and very few stories have done that.

Isabelle Florrie Saul's picture of the Cratchits' Christmas

Dickens and Christmas

Today's Christmas is commercial in a way that Dickens never dreamed of, but, partly thanks to him, we still feel that Christmas ought to be a time of family warmth, wholesome fun, and kindness to others, especially children. His vision lives on.

Acknowledgements

Picture Credits
The publisher would like to thank the following for their kind permission to reproduce the photographs.

t=top, b=bottom, a=above, c=centre, l=left, r=right.

AKG Photo London: 32bl; **Barnaby's Picture Library:** 8bl; **BBC Picture Library:** 61c (below); **Bridgeman Art Library:** Agnew and Sons, London 26tl; By Courtesy of the Board of the V&A 9tr, 9c, 31c (below), 31br; Central St Martin's College of Art and Design, London 14cl; Dickens House Museum, London 8cl (below), 16tl, 30tl, 61tr (below), 62cl (above); Eastgate Museum, Rochester 60br; Gavin Graham Gallery, London 7br; Guildhall Art Library, Corporation of London 6tl, 8tl, 14bl, 41tl; John Noott Galleries, Broadway, Worcester 15cr (below), 40bl; Manchester City Art Galleries 6bl; Museum of London 60c; National Gallery, London 46cl; Private Collection 22cl, 28bl, 30cl, 30/31tc, 31bc, 36tl, 37tr, 60bl, 62tl, 63br; Royal Holloway and Bedford New College, Surrey 9bl; Sheffield City Art Galleries 52cl (above); **British Museum, London:** 26cl (below); **Christie's Images, London:** 25cr, 42bl, 43br; **Dickens House Museum, London:** 60tl, 60cl, 60bl (above), 61cl, 61tr; **Mary Evans Picture Library:** 6cl, 7cr (below), 9tc(below), 11tr, 13cr (above), 14tl, 15tr, 16cl, 20tl, 20cl, 25tr, 25br, 30bl, 31tc, 31tc (below), 41cr, 41br (above), 41br, 43cr, 46tl, 47cr, 51cr, 51br, 52tl, 52cl (below), 60cl (below), 60cr, 60bc (above), 61tc, 62cl (below), 62bl, 62bc, 63tc; Arthur Rackham Collection 13br, 24bl, 50bl, 63tl (below); Explorer 20bl; **Fine Art Photographic Library:** 6br; **Hulton**

Getty: 7tr, 8tr, 8cl (above) 11br, 40tl, 50cl; **Ronald Grant Archive:** *Scrooge*, 1970 © Fox 37cr; *Scrooge*, 1935 63cr (above); *Scrooge*, 1951 © Fox 63bl; **Robert Harding Picture Library:** 29tr; C Bowman 16tl (below); David Hughs 52bl; Trevor Wood 54cl; **Illustrated London News Picture Library:** 30br, 31tr, 31cr, 57tr; Courtesy of **John Jaques and Son Ltd:** 29c (below); **Kobal Collection:** *Scrooge*, 1951 © Renown 63cr, *Little Dorrit*, Sands Films Ltd 61cr, 61br; **Billie Love Historical Collection:** 18tl, 57cr; **Museum of London:** 13cr (below), 35tr; **National Trust Photographic Library:** Andreas Von Einsiedel 13tl, 17br, 58cl; Keith Hewitt 47tr; Michael Boys 22tl; Mike Williams 29br; T Davidson 12bl; **Old House Books, Moretonhampstead, Devon:** 7tl; **Popperfoto:** 31bl; **Sotheby's Transparency Library, London:** 1c, 6c (below), 7cr, 15br, 38tl, 47br; **Tony Stone Images:** 54tl; **Tate Gallery, London:** *The Doubt - Can these Dry Bones Live?*, HA Bowler 51tr; **The Vintage Magazine Co.:** 15cr, 61c, 63tr.

Jacket: **Bridgeman Art Library:** Victoria & Albert Museum, London, inside back tc; **Sotheby's Transparency Library, London:** back cl.

Photography: Andy Crawford at the DK Studio
Additional photography: Peter Hayman, Colin Keates, Dave King, Liz McAulay, Diana Miller, David Murray & Jules Selmes, J. C. van Tol, Matthew Ward

Additional illustrations: Luigi Galante, Stephen Raw, Sallie Alane Reason

---

Dorling Kindersley would particularly like to thank the following people:

At Alfies Antique Market, London, NW8: Sandra Brunswick, Wendy Carmichael, Dudley and Genie; Angels & Bermans, London; Lizzie Bacon and Emily Edlynn for research assistance; Alastair Dougall and Nick Turpin for editorial assistance; Chris Fraser for props assistance; Sheilagh Noble for visualization.

Models: Iona Cairns, Mari Cardew-Richardson, Fergus Day, George Hobbs, Lily Kerr-Scott, Lisa Lanzarini, David Pickering, Mary Walsh, Ian Williamson
Hand model: Jane Thomas